MARC BROWN

ARTHUR'S CHICKEN POX

RED FOX

For all the chicken pox experts in Mrs Bundy's class at DeWitt Road School, with love and thanks!

A Red Fox Book

Published by Random House Children's Books
20 Vauxhall Bridge Road, London SW1V 2SA

A division of Random House UK Ltd
London Melbourne Sydney Auckland
Johannesburg and agencies throughout the world

Copyright © 1994 Marc Brown

1 3 5 7 9 10 8 6 4 2

First published in the United States of America by
Little, Brown & Company and simultaneously in Canada by
Little, Brown & Company (Canada) Ltd 1992

First published in Great Britain by Red Fox 1998

Printed in Hong Kong

RANDOM HOUSE UK Limited Reg. No. 954009

ISBN 0 09 926314 9

It was Monday morning, but Arthur's family were thinking about Saturday's trip to the circus.

"I wonder if the knife thrower will be back," said Father.

"The trapeze artists are my favourite," said Mother.

"I like the clowns best," said Arthur.

"I like the candyfloss," said D.W.

Arthur thought about the circus at school, too.

For his art project, he drew a picture of the circus.

Then at lunch time, Arthur noticed he didn't feel very well.

He went to see the school nurse.

"You've got a temperature," said the nurse.

Then Arthur's dad arrived to take him home.

"I'm going to get better fast," said Arthur. "I don't want to miss the circus."

D.W. was surprised to see Arthur when she got home from play group.

"What's wrong with you?" she asked. "You don't look very ill to me."

"But I *feel* ill," said Arthur.

"I think you're faking," said D.W.

At dinner time, Arthur was allowed to have chicken noodle soup sitting on the sofa.

"Why do I have to eat at the table?" asked D.W.

"You're not ill," said Mother.

"Well, I think Arthur is just pretending," said D.W.

"Eat your spinach," said Father.

The next morning, Arthur was *really* ill.

"Arthur's all spotty!" said D.W., laughing. "It's too bad he'll miss the circus."

"I'll see if Grandma Thora can stop by later," said Mother. "She knows all about chicken pox."

That afternoon, Grandma Thora arrived.

"I've brought you some treats to help you feel better," she said.

After school, Arthur's friends stopped by with get well cards.

Muffy brought Arthur all his homework.

Father brought Arthur some stickers and cherry-flavoured cough drops.

"Can I have a cough drop too?" asked D.W.

"You're not ill," said Arthur.

"I feel all itchy," said Arthur after dinner.

"Try not to scratch," said Grandma Thora.

"But I want to scratch," said Arthur.

"I'll make a special soothing bath," said Grandma Thora.

"That might help."

Arthur was allowed to drink juice in the bathtub with a crazy
straw.

"If you're a good boy and don't scratch your spots," said D.W.,

"I'll bring you home a balloon from the circus."

After his bath, Grandma Thora gave Arthur a back rub and told him a story.

"I think I'm ready for my hot lemon drink now," said Arthur.
"And don't forget the extra honey! Please!"
"Can I have a back rub, too?" asked D.W.
"Maybe later," said Grandma Thora. "Right now I've got to get Arthur's drink."
Suddenly, D.W. had an idea.

She went into the bathroom and closed the door.

First D.W. put baby powder on her face to look pale.

Then she looked through her box of pens for a pink one.

And she gave herself spots – lots of spots.

D.W. made loud moaning sounds as she came down the stairs.
"I don't feel well," she said.
"Good heavens," said Grandma Thora. "Now you've got spots,
too! Let me take your temperature."

When no one was looking, D.W. held the thermometer under the hot water tap.

"Oh, dear," said Grandma Thora when she read the thermometer.

"I feel itchy, too," said D.W. "I think I need a soothing bath."

"Of course," said Grandma Thora.

"And how about some juice," asked D.W., "with a crazy straw?"

"Of course, darling," said Grandma Thora.

D.W. didn't notice that while she was in the bathtub, all her
pink spots had washed right off.
But Grandma Thora noticed.
"Dora Winifred!" she scolded. "I'm very disappointed in you."

"Well, how's our little patient?" D.W. asked Arthur the nex
afternoon.

"Still itchy," said Arthur. "And still ill."

"That's too bad" said D.W.

She moved the telephone nearer to Arthur.

"Excuse me," she said. "I have to make an important call."

"Hello, Emily? I've got an extra ticket for the circus on Saturday. Want to go with me? . . . Great! Bye."

"Mom!" moaned Arthur. "D.W. is torturing me."

By Friday, Arthur was feeling well enough to go out to dinner with his family.

"I think I'll be going to the circus after all," he said.

"Oh, that's just grand," said Grandma Thora.

"D.W., you'd better call Emily," said Mother.

"Maybe I should wait," said D.W. "Who knows? Arthur might get the flu."

But Arthur didn't get the flu.

The next morning, he was up early and dressed for the circus

Everyone else was ready for the circus, too.

Everyone except D.W.

"Hurry up, D.W., or we'll be late," called Mother.

D.W. came down the stairs singing, "It's candyfloss I love to eat.

It's so squishy. It's so sweet."

Mother just looked at D.W.

"Oh, boy," said Father.

"Good heavens," said Grandma Thora.
Arthur started laughing.
"What's so funny?" asked D.W.

"Back to bed, young lady," said Mother.

"But what about the circus?" cried D.W.

"Don't worry," said Arthur. "If you're a good little girl and don't scratch, I'll bring you home a balloon."